Finders Keepers for Franklin

Text © 1997 Contextx Inc.
Illustrations © 1997 Brenda Clark Illustrator Inc.

Interior illustrations prepared with the assistance of Shelley Southern.

This edition is only available for distribution through the school market by Scholastic Canada Book Fairs and Book Clubs.

ISBN 978-1-77138-143-7

CM PA 13 0 9 8 7 6 5 4 3 2 1

Kids Can Press acknowledges the financial support of the Ontario Arts Council; the Canada Council for the Arts and the Government of Canada, through the CBF, for our publishing activity.

Published in Canada by
Kids Can Press Ltd.
25 Dockside Drive
Toronto, ON M5A 0B5

Published in the U.S. by
Kids Can Press Ltd.
2250 Military Road
Tonawanda, NY 14150

www.kidscanpress.com

The hardcover edition of this book is smyth sewn casebound.
The paperback edition of this book is limp sewn with a drawn-on cover.
Manufactured in Buji, Shenzhen, China, in 11/2013 by WKT Company

CM 97 0 9 8 7 6 5 4 3 2
CDN PA 97 0 9 8 7 6 5 4
CMC PA 13 0 9 8 7 6 5 4 3 2 1

Library and Archives Canada Cataloguing in Publication

Bourgeois, Paulette
    Finders keepers for Franklin / written by Paulette Bourgeois ; illustrated by Brenda Clark.

(A classic Franklin story)
ISBN 978-1-77138-003-4

    1. Franklin (Fictitious character : Bourgeois) — Juvenile fiction.
I. Clark, Brenda II. Title. III. Series: Classic Franklin story

PS8553.O85477F55 2013   jC813'.54   C2012-907876-X

Kids Can Press is a *l*©r**u**s™ Entertainment company

Finders Keepers for Franklin

Written by Paulette Bourgeois
Illustrated by Brenda Clark

Kids Can Press

FRANKLIN could count by twos and tie his shoes. He was good at seeing things that others missed. Once Franklin found a lucky four-leaf clover. Another time, he found the keys his mother had lost. But one day Franklin found something special.

Franklin was walking to the park when he spotted a flash of blue. Something was lying by the side of the path.

"Oh!" said Franklin, picking it up. "A camera!"

He had never found anything quite so wonderful before.

Franklin looked through the viewfinder.
He imagined he was a photographer, just like
Grandma, who took last summer's pictures.
    "Say 'Cheese!'" he said.
    Franklin pretended to click the clicker.
    Then he noticed that somebody had already
taken one picture.

As soon as Franklin got to the park, he showed the camera to his friends.

"Wow," said Moose. "Is that yours?"

"Not exactly," said Franklin. "I found it."

Beaver shrugged. "Finders keepers," she said.

"Well, I looked, but there's no name on the camera," said Franklin.

"Then it's yours," insisted Beaver.

"It's not like stealing," said Moose. "You found it."

Still, Franklin knew he wasn't allowed to keep things that didn't belong to him.

He decided to find the owner later.

Just then, Beaver made a funny face.
"That's good!" said Franklin.
He snapped a picture.

"Me too! Me too!" cried Moose and Rabbit.
Before he knew it, Franklin had used the
rest of the film.

Franklin took the film out of the camera and put it in his marble bag.

"I'll have to get more film," he said.

"Are you keeping the camera?" asked Moose.

Franklin looked surprised.

"Whoops! I almost forgot that it isn't mine," said Franklin. "I'd better find out who lost it."

"Maybe the owner will be mad because you used the camera," Beaver said.

Franklin gulped. "I didn't think of that."

Now Franklin wasn't sure what to do. He
didn't like it when someone was angry with him.

Franklin thought for a while.

After his friends left, he put the camera back
where he'd found it.

"That's better," he sighed. "Now nobody will be
mad at me."

Franklin went home and ate a nice supper.

After supper, Franklin's father wanted to play marbles. When Franklin opened his marble bag, the film rolled out.

"What's that?" asked Franklin's father.

"Ummm," said Franklin.

His father waited patiently.

Finally, Franklin blurted out the whole story — finding the camera, using it and then putting the camera back.

"So you used something that didn't belong to you?" asked his father.

"Not on purpose," answered Franklin. "It just sort of happened."

"What do you think should happen now?" said his father.

Franklin thought and thought.

"Maybe we could get the camera and try to find the owner," he said finally.

So Franklin and his father got the camera, made signs and posted them in the park.

They waited a week, but nobody claimed the camera.

Then they went to the police station and told the officers that they'd found a camera. Still nobody claimed it.

Franklin took the film to be developed. He bought a new roll of film with his allowance and popped it into the camera.

The next day, the pictures were ready.
Franklin held up a photo of Raccoon's family.
"I know who owns the camera!" he shouted.
"Raccoon must have taken a picture just before
he lost the camera. And he's been away, so he
didn't see our signs."

Franklin returned the camera to Raccoon and apologized for using his film.

Raccoon wasn't mad at all. He was so happy to have his camera back that he shared his snack with Franklin.

"Cheese!" said Franklin, smiling.

And Raccoon snapped a picture.